Joyful Black Child

The Adventures of Mya and Malik:

MY WORDS ARE SUPERPOWERS

Written by Porsha Hargrove

Affirming Black Voices, LLC
P.O Box 691
Glenn Dale, MD 20769
www.affirmingblackvoices.com

Printed in the United States of America

First Printing, 2017

ISBN 978-0-9988316-0-2

To My Mother:

Thank you for the life lessons you taught me. You taught me how to love myself and how to love others unconditionally. You taught me how to give, even if I have nothing left to give. Your spirit of compassion showed me how to find the hidden blessing inside every burden, and how to allow life difficulties to strengthen me. Mommy, you spoke life into me every day. Those words shaped me and allowed me to see the light at the end of every tunnel. Through this book series, your legacy shall live on forever.

I miss you and I will always love you.

This book is also dedicated to:

My nieces Jaylan, Tayler, and Quinn; my nephew Christopher, and my god-daughter Brielle.
You are all beautiful, bright, and powerful beyond measure. Never let others dim your light.

Every morning before Mya and Malik begin their day, they burst into their parents' room and hop up onto their bed. Mommy and Daddy always laugh and give them warm hugs and kisses!

Mommy smiles and says "Are you ready for a great day?" "Yes!" they scream.

Mya and Malik love their time with mommy and daddy in the morning. It makes them feel good on the inside. Mya and Malik sit on the bed and wait for Mommy to begin their morning affirmations.

"Let's begin!" Mommy says.

Together the whole family says, "I am kind and caring. I am strong in my mind, in my body and in my heart. I love my brown skin. I am beautiful, bold and brilliant! I am grateful for what I have and I will help people who aren't as fortunate as I am. I will always work hard and do my best."

Then mommy says, "There is no such thing as what?"

Mya and Malik say, "There is no such thing as failure, only lessons learned." Then daddy says, "What do you do when you fall down?"

"Dust yourself off and try again! Today will be a great day!" They scream, smiling and jumping up and down.

After their morning affirmations, Mya and Malik eat breakfast and get dressed. On Saturday mornings they go outside to play. One Saturday morning, after breakfast was over, Mya sat in the kitchen waiting for Malik and trying to think of something fun to do. Malik walked into the kitchen with something in his hand that Mya had never seen before.

"Hey Mya, do you want to help me with my experiment?" Malik asked. "I'm making a lava lamp."
"Wow Malik, that looks really cool! Let me see!" Mya said. She quickly yanked the glass jar from Malik.

"Mya, wait!" Malik said, but it was too late. The glass jar slipped out of Mya's hand, flew into the air and shattered on the kitchen floor.

"Look at what you did! You ruined it! You're so stupid," Malik shouted.

Tears welled up in Mya's eyes. Malik had never said such angry words to her before.
"Malik, I didn't mean to," Mya said.

Malik angrily yelled, "Leave me alone Mya! Instead of messing up my experiment why don't you go fix your messy hair?" Mya tried to apologize but Malik would not listen. He just stared at the shattered pieces of glass on the floor.

"Now I have to start all over again! It's going to take forever and it's all your fault!" Malik yelled at Mya as he stormed out of the kitchen

"Malik!" Mya yelled after him. "It was an accident! I'm sorry."

Mommy heard the screaming and ran into the kitchen

"Why are you two yelling?" she asked "And why is there broken glass on my kitchen floor? Are you two ok?"

"Mya ruined my experiment Mommy! She snatched it out of my hand and it broke on the floor and now I have to start all over again!"

"Cry baby," Mya whispered under her breath.

"Mya! That is not the way we talk to each other in this family! Now you apologize to your brother!" "But Mommy, I already did!" Mya said.

"Say it again," Mommy replied. "What did we tell you two about yelling at each other?"

Mya and Malik put their heads down and whispered, "Yelling doesn't make you right; it only makes you loud."

"That's right," Mommy said. "Even when you're angry it's not okay to use your words to hurt others. Do you understand?" Mommy asked.

"Yes mommy," they replied.

"Good, now go upstairs and play so I can sweep up this glass." "Yes Mommy," they said.

Mya and Malik went upstairs to play. Malik went into his room and sat on his bed to think. He didn't like to fight with his sister and was sorry for the angry words he'd said to her. Malik walked quietly into Mya's room.

"Hey, Mya. Do you want to go outside and play?"

"No," Mya said.

"Well, do you want to play a game?" Malik asked.

Mya looked at him and said, "Why would you want to play with someone stupid with messy hair?" Malik put his head down. "I didn't mean that Mya."

"Why did you say it if you didn't mean it?" Mya asked angrily. "You really hurt my feelings!" "I know Mya. I'm really sorry," Malik said.

"I won't magically feel better just because you said sorry Malik!" Mya said before storming out of the room, headed for the backyard.

Malik watched her walk away and wished he could take back his angry words.

Mya walked over to the garden where Mommy had planted African violets. Mya loved to look at them in their beautiful colors of purple and pink. Usually just looking at them made her happy. But today even their beautiful colors couldn't lift her mood.

"If only I could be as pretty as the flowers," she said to herself. "They're beautiful and strong. They aren't stupid or messy like me." She put her head down and began to cry, thinking about the words Malik had said to her. The more she thought of those words, the more she believed them. The more she believed them, the worse she felt. The worse she felt, the harder she cried. She reached up and touched her hair. Maybe it was a little messy. She thought about how she'd broken Malik's lava lamp. Maybe she was stupid.

"Malik is good at lots of things, like Math and Science," she said "I'm horrible at Math! All I can do is play the violin and write stories – and that's boring! I'll never be as good as Malik! I guess I'll just be stupid, messy Mya."

Mya continued to sit beside the African Violets, talking to herself about all the things that were wrong with her. While she talked she noticed something strange. As she said negative things about herself, the violets began to wither.

"I'm an awful sister," she said, "I destroyed all of Malik's hard work!"

Right in front of her eyes the beautiful purple flower petals turned brown and fell off of their stems. The more she spoke, the more petals began to litter the ground beneath the flowers. By the time she was done talking all of the petals had fallen off.

Mya began to reach for the flowers. She was so sad! The African Violets were her favorite thing about the backyard and now they were dying!

While Mya sat crying, worrying about the flowers, daddy silently walked up behind her, leaned down and whispered in her ear, "Hey ladybug," Daddy said, "How's my favorite girl?"

"Not so good Daddy." Mya said sadly

"You know what sometimes helps when we have 'not so good' days?" Daddy asked, "A nice, yummy dinner!" Daddy said, patting his belly. "And it smells like Mommy made an especially yummy one today!"

Daddy reached out his hand. Mya took it and followed him into the house, looking back at the flowers and wondering what to do.

Malik, Mya, Mommy and Daddy loved dinner time. It was when they prayed, laughed and spent time together. But tonight was different.

Mya and Malik sat quietly with their heads down, both picking at their food. Mommy and Daddy knew something was wrong. "Kids, you're both awfully quiet this evening. What's on your minds?" Daddy asked.

"Nothing," Mya and Malik replied in unison.

"Nothing looks like something," Daddy said, "What's going on?"

As tears rolled down her face, Mya put her hands in her lap. She felt so bad. She didn't even want to look at Daddy. "I ruined Malik's experiment. Now he hates me," Mya said,

"I don't hate you Mya!" Malik said.

Mya turned to Malik, her face twisted with anger and sadness, "Well if you don't hate me why did you call me stupid?" "I already said I was sorry Mya!" Malik shouted.

Mya ignored Malik and looked back at her lap. "It doesn't matter anyway." Mya continued. "I even made the violets in the backyard die. Everything I touch gets ruined!"

Mommy and Daddy looked at each other and then back at Mya and Malik.
"Mya, come with me for a minute."

Daddy took Mya into the living room and stood her in front of the mirror. "Take a look in this mirror and tell me what you see." Daddy said.

Mya looked into the mirror and put her head down. "Just me Daddy. Just plain old Mya with messy hair."

Daddy put his hand on her shoulder and smiled.

"Well you know what I see? I see a smart, talented little girl. She has beautiful brown skin and her eyes twinkle like the stars. Her hair, well, her hair is her crown. No matter how she wears it, it is beautiful, thick and strong!

Mya considered the mirror and tried to see what Daddy saw. She put her hand to her hair and smiled. Maybe Daddy was right. Maybe she was smart and talented and strong!

Mya turned and gave Daddy a big hug and kiss.

"Thank you Daddy! You're the best!" Mya said

While daddy talked to Mya, Mommy looked across the table at Malik.
"Malik, baby what's wrong?" Mommy asked.

"Mya won't play with me. She's still mad at me for calling her stupid," Malik said staring down at his lap. "I didn't mean it Mommy. I was just mad at her for messing up my experiment."

"What have Daddy and I always told you about your words Malik?" Malik shrugged. He was too sad to answer.

"Your words have power in them." Mommy said softly. "Your words can build people up or tear them down. They can make someone feel happy or sad, encouraged or defeated." Malik nodded.

"It's ok to be mad, but you can't use your words to hurt people out of anger."

"I'm sorry Mommy." Malik said. "From now on I'm going to be more careful of what I say because I don't want to hurt anyone's feelings. Especially Mya's. She's my best friend!"

Mommy smiled at Malik. "I think you owe Mya an apology," she said. "Okay Mommy. I'm going to find just the right words to say to her!"

"Malik, it's not easy to admit when you've been wrong. I'm very proud of you! You are growing into to such an amazing young man," Mommy said.

"May I be excused?" Malik asked, "I want to go and talk to Mya." "Sure you can," Mommy said, "Good luck!" Malik looked at Mommy with a smile. "I won't need luck! I've got my words…and they have superpowers!"

Malik ran happily from the room.

Malik peeked around the corner and saw Daddy talking to Mya while she stood in front of the mirror. He boldly walked over and said, "Hi Daddy! Hi Mya."

"Hey son," daddy replied. "Mya just told me what happened."
Malik stood in front of his sister.

"Mya, I have something to tell you. I'm so sorry for the mean things I said to you. You're not stupid Mya, you're really smart and talented! I wish that I could play the violin like you do, or write such awesome stories! And you're the only third grader I know who reads better than the sixth graders!"

Malik smiled at Mya and continued. "I know I said your hair was messy but I didn't mean it. I like your hair! I only said those things because I was angry. But now I know how important my words are. I'll never talk to you that way again."

Mya was so happy to hear Malik's words.

"Malik, I'm sorry too! I didn't mean to ruin your experiment. It was an accident. I was just so excited to help! I should have been more careful. Please forgive me," Mya shared.

"I forgive you Mya," Malik said.

"Malik and Mya, I'm very proud of both of you," Dad replied. "Now how about hugging it out?"
Malik and Mya laughed and hugged each other.

"Alright you two, back to the kitchen so we can finish dinner," Daddy said.

"Kids, I'm happy you two worked out your problems," Daddy said, "Your mother and I are very proud of you."

"Thank you Daddy!" Malik said, "Now I know that my words are superpowers so I have to be careful how I used them, right Mommy?"

"That's right Malik," Mommy said.

Daddy turned to Mya, who still looked a little troubled.

"Mya, what did you say about the plants in the backyard?" Daddy asked

"I ruined them," Mya said, "I sat by them and every time I spoke they just withered and died."
"Why don't we all go take a look?" Daddy said.

Everyone headed to the backyard and gathered around the flower bed.

"See daddy," Mya said. "They're all withered. Their beautiful petals have all fallen off and I didn't even touch them! I only talked about what happened earlier today."

"What exactly did you say?" Daddy asked.

"I don't know," Mya replied. "Something like, 'I'm the worst and I must be stupid'."

Daddy looked at the flowers and then at Mya. "Kids do you know the saying sticks and stones may break my bones but words will never hurt me?" Daddy asked.

"Yes," Mya and Malik responded.

"Well that isn't really the whole truth," Daddy said. "The truth is that our thoughts and words are very powerful. When you speak negative words, think negative thoughts and have negative feelings it can damage all the good things in your life. Mya, how did Malik's words make you feel this morning?"

"They made me feel really bad," Mya said. "But after he said sorry I felt much better."

"That's right Mya," Daddy said, "Positive words and thoughts will always be more powerful than negative ones."

"But what about the flowers Daddy?" Mya said, "Will they ever grow back?"

Daddy stood with mommy beside the flower bed. He looked down at Mya and Malik. "I have an idea," Daddy said, "Mya, didn't you say that the flowers withered when you spoke negatively?"

"Yes, Daddy," Mya said.

"Well then, why don't we try something? Let's try speaking positive words!" Daddy said, "Mya and Malik, repeat after me." Standing in the garden with Mommy and Daddy, Mya and Malik said:

"I AM STRONG
I AM POWERFUL
I AM BEAUTIFUL
I AM INTELLIGENT
I AM WORTHY
MY LIFE MATTERS!"

As they said each phrase the flowers miraculously began to come back to life. They stood, strong and tall, even more beautiful than they'd been before.

"Look! Look! The petals are coming back!" Mya exclaimed.

"Well will you look at that!" Mommy said. "See, your words are powerful!"

"Wow! What I say is important!" Mya said. "Thank you Mommy and Daddy! Thank you for helping me learn that my words really are superpowers!"

My Words Are Superpowers Activity

Help Malik finish his experiment by making a Homemade Lava Lamp
(Adult supervision required)

MATERIALS:

Clear plastic bottle
Vegetable oil or baby oil
Water
Food coloring
Alka-Seltzer tablets

DIRECTIONS:

1. Pour water into the plastic bottle until it is around one quarter full (use a funnel when filling the bottle so you don't spill anything).
2. Pour in vegetable oil/baby oil until the bottle is nearly full.
3. Wait until the oil and water have separated.
4. Add around 5-10 drops of food coloring to the bottle (choose your favorite color).
5. Watch as the food coloring falls through the oil and mixes with the water.
6. Cut an Alka-Seltzer tablet into smaller pieces (around 5 or 6) and drop one of them into the bottle, you should see activity, just like a real lava lamp!
7. When the bubbling stops, add another piece of Alka-Seltzer and enjoy the show!

I would like to express my gratitude to the many people who saw me through this book. Thank you to all those who provided support through prayer, feedback, reviews, edits, and the design of this project. God placed a vision in my spirit; because of you, my dreams have manifested into reality.

Holland Hargrove

Tressa Azarel

Melodye Hunter

Adebayo Adegbembo

PhiXavier Holmes, M.Ed

Dawshawn Taylor

D.C. Miles

Ayanna Johnson

Shauna Knox, M.Ed

Brittany Smotherson, M.Ed

Janita Butler, M.Ed

Marika Martin Ph.D., LCMFT, CFLE

Narlie Bedney, LCPC

Daun Duncan

Ceara Flake, Esq.

Anthony Duncan Jr. Esq.

Brittany Butler, Ph.D

Candice Cannon-Chilton

Christopher Chilton

Da Crew

Tara Seals, MSN, CPNP

Brittny Johnson

Affirming Black Voices

Joyful Black Child

The Adventures of Mya and Malik:

MY WORDS ARE SUPERPOWERS

Written by Porsha Hargrove